FROOBIE PINK
AND THE NIGHT NOISES

For Lisa
For having faith

A Red Fox Book

Published by Random House Children's Books
20 Vauxhall Bridge Road, London SW1V 2SA

A division of The Random House Group Ltd
London Melbourne Sydney Auckland
Johannesburg and agencies throughout the world

Copyright © Stephen Hanson 2000

1 3 5 7 9 10 8 6 4 2

First published in Great Britain by
Red Fox 2000

Printed in Hong Kong

Papers used by The Random House Group Ltd are natural,
recyclable products made from wood grown in sustainable forests.
The manufacturing processes conform to the
environmental regulations of the country of origins.

The Random House Group Limited Reg. No. 954009

www.randomhouse.co.uk

ISBN 0 09 940445 1

FROOBIE PINK
AND THE NIGHT NOISES

STEPHEN HANSON

RED FOX

F roobie Pink lay in bed
and listened as his
grandma read him
a story.

Outside, the sky
turned dark and the
thunder GROWLED and
RUMBLED. Froobie hid
under the bedclothes.

"Don't be scared of the
storm, Froobie," said
Grandma Pink, holding his
hand tight. "The rain, the
lightning and the thunder
are all outside. They can't
hurt you."

But Froobie was frightened of all the night noises. He could hear them even with his head under the pillow.

"Close your eyes and count to fifty," said Grandma, "and the thunder will have gone. You'll see."

Froobie counted. When he reached fifty, he listened hard. All was quiet. Grandma Pink had been right.

But seconds later the noises were back. The rain PITTER- PATTERED, the lightning CRACKED and the thunder GROWLED. Slowly Froobie opened his eyes. Grandma was gone, and he was alone with the noises.

Suddenly there was a RATTLE at the window, then a TAP-TAP-TAP, then a BANG, BANG, BANG...

...BANG,
WHOOSH!
The window
burst open and
in blew the wind
with a HOWL,
swirling round and
round the room. Froobie
cried out to his grandma
but she didn't hear. With
a swish, Froobie and his
bed were swept off the floor,
and carried out through the
window into the night sky.

Higher and higher they flew, above the houses and trees and up into the clouds. Froobie peeped down and saw his grandma's house, tiny in the distance. Then it disappeared altogether as they flew into a big, black cloud. At last the wind stopped blowing, and Froobie's bed landed without a sound.

Froobie stood very still.
As he gazed around, a little
man suddenly appeared out
of the mist.

"Thank you for coming,
Froobie," said Mr Chillyweather.
"We really need your help.
The Noises are all so scared."

Froobie was scared too, but
before he could say anything,
there was an almighty CRASH.

"Come out, CRASH,"
said Mr Chillyweather,
"and meet Froobie."

Froobie watched
as a very small and
nervous-looking creature
emerged out of the mist.

"Pleased to meet you,"
it whispered.

Froobie was amazed.
CRASH wasn't scary at all.
Very slowly, more creatures
appeared. Froobie smiled
shyly as Mr Chillyweather
introduced PITTER-
PATTER, RUSTLE and
CRACK.

"Thank you for coming
to help us," they cried.

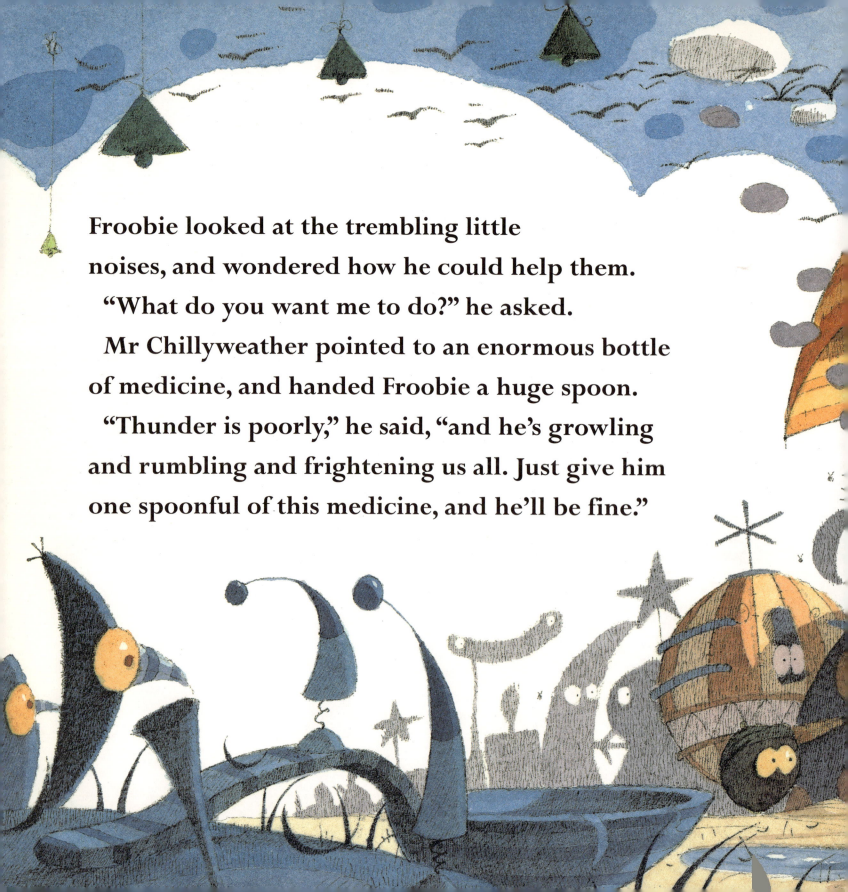

Froobie looked at the trembling little
noises, and wondered how he could help them.

"What do you want me to do?" he asked.

Mr Chillyweather pointed to an enormous bottle
of medicine, and handed Froobie a huge spoon.

"Thunder is poorly," he said, "and he's growling
and rumbling and frightening us all. Just give him
one spoonful of this medicine, and he'll be fine."

CRASH,
RUSTLE and PITTER-
PATTER poured the gooey,
yellow potion into the spoon,
and placed it on Froobie's bed.
Froobie clambered up beside it, and with
a swish, the bed took off into the night.
"But where is Thunder?" Froobie shouted.
"We're standing on him!" called
Mr Chillyweather. "Good luck!"

Froobie clung on tight as the bed sailed through the black, misty sky. All he could hear was the deep RUMBLE of Thunder, growing louder and louder. Then the mist suddenly lifted. Froobie forced himself to look, and there in front of him...

...was an enormous beak and two large sleepy eyes!

Froobie let out a terrified scream. But as the bed moved closer to the huge beak, he saw that Thunder looked very poorly and tired. Froobie felt rather sorry for the creature. He took a deep breath and smiled nervously.

"I have some medicine for you," he shouted as loudly as he could. "Please could you open wide?"

Slowly Thunder opened his huge, creaking jaws. Froobie gulped. There was no turning back now. He stepped on to the long, spotty tongue and tip-toed between the rows of sharp teeth.

But as he neared the end the great mouth began to GROWL and RUMBLE.

"Ahh-ahh," wheezed Thunder.

Froobie froze. He was about to be caught in an enormous sneeze.

"Ahh-ahh," Thunder spluttered.

Without stopping to think Froobie popped in the medicine and turned and fled.

"CHOO!" sneezed Thunder.

The blast sent Froobie hurtling through the air...

...until he landed back on his bed with a bounce. The bed sprung into action, spinning round and round.

A moment later Froobie was back in his bedroom.

The growl of Thunder had gone. Froobie
ran downstairs and out into the garden.
A wonderful sight awaited him.

Froobie fell asleep thinking about the gentle
Noises. He knew he would never be scared of
the night noises again, even Thunder. And as
Froobie dreamed, Mr Chillyweather left him a
gift. It was a beautiful, shiny medal which said,
    'To Froobie, for Braving the Storm.'